P9-DTO-868

LITTLE RED HOODIE

LITTLE RED HOODIE

◄───◆───►

Martha Freeman

illustrated by
Marta Sevilla

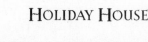HOLIDAY HOUSE · NEW YORK

Library of Congress Cataloging-in-Publication Data
Names: Freeman, Martha, 1956- author. | Sevilla, Marta (Illustrator), illustrator.
Title: Little Red Hoodie / by Martha Freeman ; illustrations by Marta Sevilla.
Description: First edition. | New York : Holiday House, [2020] | Audience:
Ages 7-10. | Audience: Grades 4-6. | Summary: Fairy tale characters help
Little Red Hoodie find the thief who stole her basket of goodies.
Identifiers: LCCN 2019026084 | ISBN 9780823446216 (hardcover)
Subjects: CYAC: Characters in literature—Fiction. | Humorous stories.
Classification: LCC PZ7.F87496 Li 2020 | DDC [Fic]—dc23
LC record available at https://lccn.loc.gov/2019026084

For Joyce Manning, my favorite aunt,
whose humor, generosity, and pluck
inspire so many people.

CONTENTS

PROLOGUE

A Knock at the Door

Once upon a time there were three bears.

You are a character in the story.

The main character in the story?

Not exactly.

And who exactly is the main character?

Exactly me! Bobby Bear!

Now, where was I?

Oh, yeah.

Once upon a time there were three bears, and they lived together happily in a tidy cottage in the woods.

One day, Bobby Bear, the main character of the story, was making his bed when he heard a knock at the door.

Well, you are, kind of.

So sorry. But didn't you already have a go at being the main character in the previous installment?

Just once I'd like to tell a story without all these interruptions.

That would require you to tell the story correctly. May I give it a try?

Sure, go ahead. Take a turn telling the story. If I've learned anything about humans, it's that they don't give you a moment's peace until you say yes.

ONE

What Even Is an Arthropod?

Once upon a time

there was a nice little girl who lived with her mother in a nice little village surrounded by nice woods.

> Do you know any adjectives besides "nice"?

I am being accurate. Everything was very nice. Until it wasn't.

Hmmm. Suspenseful.

The nice little girl is the main character of the story.

Of this chapter, you mean.

To protect her from wind and weather—and because she liked the color—this nice little girl, the main character, always wore a red sweatshirt with a hood. After a while her friends gave her a nickname, Little Red Hoodie.

There is one additional thing you should know about this nice little girl: she really, really, really liked arthropods.

Arthropods . . . what? What even is an arthropod?

Insects and spiders, lobsters, crawfish, and crabs are all arthropods.

Ewww! Why did she like them?

Her whole family did. It all started with her great aunt, Miss Muffet, who overcame her childhood fear of spiders and went on to become an expert.

But what could a person possibly like about spiders and other—what did you call them?

Arthropods. And what she liked about them was everything!

The way their legs and antennae wiggle. The way their big compound eyes see up, down, and sideways all at once. The way their spiracles let air flow in and out; the way they shed their exoskeletons anytime they need to grow.

> If you say so. But more importantly, how did she feel about bears?

I suppose that depends on the bear, doesn't it?

One nice morning in the village, Little Red Hoodie's mama asked her to carry a basket of goodies to her grandmother, who had just moved to a new cottage.

> You mean like a housewarming gift?

Precisely.

But why didn't Little Red Hoodie's mama go with her?

Because she had to work, silly. I don't know how it is in the woods, but out in the burbs where I live, most mamas have jobs besides mama.

What job did Little Red Hoodie's mama have?

Banana bread baker.

I love banana bread.

Everyone does.

It was a beautiful morning, and Little Red Hoodie was excited to be embarking on an adventure. But she was also just a tad bit concerned.

"Mama," she said, "you do realize I'm directionally challenged, right?"

"You mean you get lost a lot? Yes, I know. But you've been to your grandmother's old cottage many times, and the new cottage is only a hop, skip, and a jump away. Besides, I've drawn you a map."

Red Hoodie took the basket from her mama. Together they looked at the map while Mama traced the route.

"Follow Magic Wand Lane to Glass Slipper Boulevard, right on Beanstalk, left on Breadcrumb, down the Garden Path, and you're there," said Mama.

It's possible that Little Red Hoodie was not paying 100 percent attention. It's possible that Little Red Hoodie instead was thinking of an extra goodie to add to the basket.

"Do you understand?" Mama asked.

"What?" said Red. "Oh, certainly, Mama. Hop, skip, jump. Garden path. I've got it."

"Hmmm," said Mama. "And one thing more. Do not cross the bridge that's guarded by the troll. Beyond it are the scary woods where anything might happen. Do you remember the story of Goldilocks?"

Story of Goldilocks? Don't you mean the story of Bobby Bear?

Call it what you will, the story of Goldilocks's safe return from the woods had gone viral. Everyone in the burbs knew it well.

"Don't worry, Mama," she said. "I am going to follow your map to Grandma's house, and nothing bad will happen."

Which is not quite the way it turned out.

TWO

Something Much Worse Than a Troll

You will remember that Red had an idea for a goodie for her grandma? Shortly before she left home, she added it to the basket. The goodie was something special in the way of home décor, something Little Red knew her grandmother would love.

So what was it, anyway?

Patience, my good bear. All will be revealed in time.

For now, Red skipped off down the lane. Not wanting to end up like Goldilocks, she stopped frequently and consulted the map.

Unfortunately, there was one little problem.

She was holding the map upside down.

In time she came to a bridge that crossed a brook. "Oh dear," she thought. "Could this be the bridge Mama warned me about? The one that's guarded by a troll?"

Confused and uncertain, Red started across. She was about halfway when she heard commotion below her and then the bleated words: "Who goes there?"

"It's I, Little Red Hoodie. Please tell me you're not a troll!"

Trip-trop, trip-trop, trip-trop came the sound of hooves on the wooden bridge, then a small barnyard creature blocked her path. It had floppy ears, a long beard, and very pointy horns.

"Do I look like a troll?" it asked.

"You look like a billy goat," said Red, very much relieved. Obviously, this was not the troll's bridge after all.

Yes, it was. But the troll who used to guard it lost his job for letting intruders into the woods.

Yes, yes, I know that now, but I didn't know it then. And neither did Mama.

That's what happens when you don't keep up with current events.

"I am the smallest Billy Goat Gruff," said the goat. "Very good to know you. Say, what've you got in your hand there?"

"A basket full of goodies for my grandma," said Red.

"Not that hand, the other one," said the goat.

Red realized he meant Mama's map and held it out so he could see. Quick as a wink, he snatched it in his teeth and ate it up.

"Hey!" Red cried.

"Where?" The goat looked around. "Hay would make a fine dessert."

"I meant, 'Hey, you ate my map!'" said Little Red.

"No worries," said the goat. "You're taking that basket to Grandma? She's human, I bet, and only one human lives around here. Follow the path, and then keep going. Long walk. Big house. No way you can miss it."

Little Red Hoodie's mama had mentioned a path. This must be the same one. The goat's directions were simple. Surely even she could follow them.

Secretly hoping the map gave the goat a stomachache, Little Red Hoodie said goodbye, and departed down the path.

"Sure are a lot of trees," she thought. "You'd almost think this was the woods. But it's not scary at all. It's nice."

Little Red Hoodie liked the chirp and chitter of live things all around. She wondered if jumping spiders, with their excellent eyesight, were watching her, or if arrowhead spiders were busy above her, spinning morning webs.

But Red's happy thoughts soon were interrupted by a big, bad voice that seemed to come out of nowhere: "What's that I see on the path? Looks like brunch to me! And if my nose is not mistaken, banana bread for dessert!"

Poor Red was so startled she almost jumped out of her boots. "Wh-Wh-Who's there? Oh boy, I hope you're not a troll."

"Not at all," said the voice, "I'm something much worse than a troll!" And out of the trees came a shiny-pelted, red-eyed, fearsome-looking—

Thanks awfully, but I believe I can handle this on my own.

You're doing swell so far. First your map's upside down. Then you cross the bridge your mama tells you to stay away from. Now you're about to be eaten by a wolf!

So I won't hire out as a wilderness guide. May I continue?

Be my guest.

As I was saying, it was the Wolf!

"Greetings, fair maiden," he said. "Is that banana bread you've got in the basket? I love banana bread."

Little Red Hoodie replied politely, "I am on my way to visit my grandma. Your keen nose is right about banana bread. Other than that, only goodies in the basket. That's all. Just goodies."

Lips smacking, claws ready, the Wolf slunk closer

and closer to the trembling girl who expected any moment to be gobbled up.

But then—abruptly—the Wolf stopped in his tracks. "Do you hear something?" he asked.

Red saw her chance. "Look there, Mr. Wolf." She pointed. "It's a lion as big as Rhode Island! He's coming this way, and he's hungry."

The Wolf was no fan of lions. "Catch you later," he said, "and I do mean *catch*." Then away he dashed into the trees.

Now the truth of the matter is this. Red had neither heard nor seen anything at all. The big lion was entirely an invention. So, imagine her surprise when a moment later she did hear something, a *thump-thrash* sound in the undergrowth.

It seemed to be big. It seemed to be clumsy. It seemed to be coming straight for her!

May I tell another chapter?

Thank you very much, Bear. And now, dear reader, please turn the page.

THREE

Where's the Drama in That?

Once again, Little Red Hoodie stood trembling on the path. Had she saved herself from the Wolf only to be eaten by something worse?

On the other hand, if you're going to be eaten, does it really matter what does the eating?

Very possibly not. But at that moment Red was too busy trembling to think super-clearly, and then—*bleat!*—the latest threat's true identity was revealed. It had floppy ears, a long beard, and very pointy horns.

Another billy goat!

This one was one size larger and, horns down, it came trotting toward Red on the path.

Red remembered library story hour . . . and that's when she understood. "You must be the middle-sized Billy Goat Gruff!"

"At your service," said the goat.

"You came along at a lucky time for me," Red said, and she explained about meeting the Wolf.

"Pay me back in banana bread," said the goat. "I've been following the scent ever since you left the bridge."

Red said she was sorry, but she could not open her basket until she arrived at her grandmother's. "But here's an idea," she added. "I'll bring you a whole loaf of banana bread next time I'm in the neighborhood."

"Better make it two," said the second Billy Goat Gruff. "My big brother will want one for himself."

It's a lucky thing no one gobbled you up on the path.

My mama certainly thought so.

I wasn't thinking of her. I was thinking of the story! If you'd been gobbled up, there wouldn't be one.

Not much of one, it's true: Once there was a nice little girl and then there wasn't. The end.

Where's the drama in that? The conflict? The plot twists? As it was, the story continued. And I know just the good-looking young bear to tell it.

FOUR

Knock, Knock

One morning I was home making my bed, which I do every day, because that's the kind of good and careful bear I am, when I heard a knock at the door.

"Who's there?" I asked.

"We haven't actually met," came the answer, "but I'm harmless."

"How do I know?" I asked.

"I suppose you can't know for certain until (1) you open the door, and (2) you assess my person, and (3) we arm wrestle or something. Are you skilled at arm wrestling?"

"Uh . . . I don't think so," I answered. "I don't technically have arms, just forelegs."

"Oh, my gracious!" said the voice. "I never met a person with four legs before!"

"Not a person, and not four legs. *Fore*legs," I explained.

"Isn't that what I said?" the voice asked.

"No, you said four legs, as opposed to two legs. And I didn't say 'four legs.' I said '*fore*legs.' "

"Now I understand. You don't have four legs, but you do have forelegs?" the voice asked.

"Actually, I have four legs *and* forelegs," I said.

"That makes six legs, which makes you an arthropod!" said the voice outside the door. "And I am simply crazy about arthropods. Open the door so I can see."

I was picturing a talking cockroach.

23

And you got a talking bear cub instead.

No antennae, but at least you have nice mandibles.

What even are mandibles?

What you chew with. Jaws, basically.

Now, where was I? Oh yes, I opened the door and there was a furless creature—human, most likely.

"What have you done with the talking cockroach?" she asked.

"Sorry to be a disappointment," I said. "My name's

Bobby Bear. Besides being harmless, just who are you, anyway?"

"Little Red Hoodie," she replied.

"And what are you doing at my door? The last one was destructive."

"The last what?" she asked.

"The last human. Her name was Goldilocks."

"Goldilocks! You *know* her? Where I come from, she's famous!"

"What can I say? We hang out," said Bobby Bear.

"I don't think I'm destructive," said Little Red Hoodie. "What I am is lost."

I may have fearsome claws, not to mention very nice mandibles, but I am also a kindhearted guy. I stepped aside and invited the furless creature in. "Nice basket," I said. "What's in it? Smells like banana bread."

"It is banana bread, along with other goodies for my grandmother," she said. "There's nothing else in the basket. Goodies. Only goodies."

"For your grandmother?" I said. "Whoa—when you say lost, you aren't kidding. Either you're in the wrong woods altogether, or else the wrong fairytale. Only one human lives around here, and she isn't anyone's grandmother. She is an evil queen."

FIVE

Maybe You're Evil, Too!

I **begged** to disagree.

"Begged to disagree." That's really the way she talks! She's always hoity-toity like that.

Some might say "classy."

Some might. Not me, but some.

"It seems to me," I continued, "that since my grandmother is human, and the evil queen is the only human who lives nearby, then my grandmother must be the evil queen."

Bobby Bear's eyes grew wide. "Yikes! Then what does that make you?"

"I don't mean that she's really evil," I said. "I think it's likely there's been some misunderstanding."

"Or," said Bobby, "maybe *you're* evil, too. Did you ever think of that? I mean, you do like spiders."

"Spiders are not evil," I said.

"Some of them are at least. Black widows eat their husbands," said Bobby.

"It's impolite to comment on food choices," I said.

"Maybe," said Bobby, "but I know a guy named Big Bad Wolf. Given half a chance, his food choices would include you."

"I know him, too," I said. "We met this morning on the path."

"No way! Then how come you're even here? "

I told Bobby Bear what had happened. Bobby Bear wouldn't admit it, but he was impressed with my quick thinking.

That's when Mama Bear and Papa Bear came in.

"Why Baby—that is, *Bobby* Bear—another little furless friend? How charming!" said Mama. "Shall I fix us all some porridge?"

"Thanks ever so," I said. "But I must be on my way." And I explained my errand.

Papa Bear shook his head. "It's not safe for you to be alone in the woods. Have you ever heard of the Big Bad Wolf?"

"Funny coincidence," said Bobby. "We were just talking about him."

"I see your point, but I'm in rather a hurry," I said. "Banana bread only keeps so long, and . . ."

My voice trailed off because Mama Bear and Papa Bear were shaking their heads and frowning.

"No?" I said meekly.

"No," they said firmly.

"You'll stay here with us till the full moon," Papa said. "That's the wolf's night off. Bobby's room is spacious enough for company. I'm sure you'll be very comfortable."

I think my parents missed having a furless around.

What's a "furless"?

A human.

Little Red Hoodie knew that Mama and Papa were being kind. But in truth she had no time to waste. It wasn't only banana bread that wouldn't keep. The other goodies in the basket also needed to be delivered before—

Before what? I'm dying to know!

Uh . . . before anything surprising happened.

Now Little Red Hoodie was in a predicament. How to escape the bears' hospitality? She was trying to come up with a plan when, all of a sudden, she heard something *thump-thrashing* outside.

"What's that?" said Mama and Papa at once, then they raced out the back to investigate.

Bobby Bear, meanwhile, had raced to his room.

When the going gets tough, the tough hide under the bed.

Little Red Hoodie realized this was her chance and did some racing of her own: Straight out the front door and back to the path. There she realized she still had a problem. Which way was she supposed to go?

SIX

Tall. Dark. Spooky.

Hiding under my bed was a bad idea.

It was dusty and cramped, and there were cobwebs, too, and where there are cobwebs there are probably—

Spiders!

And not everybody loves spiders the way Little Red Hoodie does.

They should, though.

So I crawled out in a hurry and returned to the parlor and discovered that Mama and Papa and Little Red
Hoodie were gone!

Since the scary *thump-thrash* had come from out back, I went out the front. And there by the path, I found Little Red. She was as lost as ever.

"Oh, Bobby Bear," she said. "I can't stay with your family until the full moon. My grandma needs her goodies, and my mama would worry. Won't you tell me how to get to the queen's house?""

"I'll tell you," I said, "but I'm not saying it's a good idea. What you do is make a right here, go around the pond, pass Coyote's den, go over the mountain, go down to the valley, watch out for flying monkeys, and—ta da!—you're at the castle. Tall. Dark. Spooky. You'll know it when you see it."

"Somehow I was picturing more like a humble cottage with roses and a vegetable garden," Red said.

"Nope. Tall, dark, spooky. I've been there. I know."

"You've been there?" she asked.

"With Goldilocks," I said.

"Then maybe you could come with me," said Little Red. "Please? You don't have to meet my grandmother. You can wait outside. It's just that I'm directionally challenged, and I'm not having the best day."

I didn't want to go.

That was obvious.

The last time I went to the castle, I'd barely escaped the clutches of the evil queen. "I've got a lot to do," I said. "Like, uh . . . take a nap. And after that I have to help with dinner."

"You help your parents make dinner?" Red asked.

"No, I help them *eat* dinner. I also help with breakfast and lunch."

Little Red Hoodie sighed. "That's okay, Bobby Bear. I understand. I can do this on my own. I go this way, right?"

I pointed the wrong way, didn't I?

You sure did. And after that, what could I do?

"Okay, fine. I'll go with you," I said. "At least maybe this time we'll avoid the crocodile."

"Crocodile?" Little Red Hoodie repeated.

SEVEN

Lights! Camera! Action!

Bobby and Red hadn't gone far when they were disturbed by yet another strange sound: *Oink! Oink! Oink!*

Red stopped and looked around. "What's that?"

Bobby stared at his new friend. "You're kidding, right? Okay, I'll give you a hint. 'Moo' says the cow, 'baaa' says the sheep, 'oink' says the . . . ?"

"I know what says 'oink,' Bobby," Red said. "I just never expected to hear it here. It's not as though Old MacDonald had a forest."

Before Bobby could reply, three pigs pushing wheel-barrows came trotting out of the shadows and onto the path ahead of them.

Red couldn't believe her eyes. "Oh my gracious—are those actually the Pig Brothers from the HoGTV? I *never* miss their home improvement show!"

"They're our next-door neighbors," Bobby said. "Come on and I'll introduce you."

But before he had the chance, there was more com-motion from the woods, and then an entire TV crew showed up hauling cables, cameras, microphones, wardrobe, makeup—the works.

While Bobby and Red watched, the crew set up equipment, makeup artists pinked the pigs' ears, and stylists curled their tails.

Bobby and Red found it all very glamorous and exciting. Then a field mouse rushed over. He was wearing gold spectacles and a straw hat. He was waving a clipboard. "Ratón Perez is my name, and teeth are my game," he said.

"Sure, I know you," said Red. "You're like the tooth fairy, only in Spanish."

The mouse twisted his whiskers. *"Exactamente,"* he said.

"But what are you doing here?" Red asked.

"Have you seen how much money kids get for teeth these days?" he asked. "I'm so broke I needed a second job. But the Pig Brothers are much too busy for autographs right now. They're studying their lines."

No, they were not. In fact, they were snout-deep in hog slops from the catering truck.

Bobby was trying to tell Señor Perez that the pigs were personal friends of his when the middle-sized one looked over and waved a trotter.

"Hey, there, neighbor!" said the pig.

"You know these guys?" Señor Perez asked the pig.

"I know Bobby, baby, sure! Son of our longtime neighbors, Mama and Papa Bear. Come on and join us for slops. Who's your friend?"

After Bobby introduced Red to his friends, Pop—

the weasel who seemed to be in charge—announced it was time to shoot the scene.

"Sorry, Bobby. We gotta get back to work," said the biggest pig. "Feel free to stick around and watch if you want."

"I got a better idea," said Pop. "We could use some extras in the background. Cute woodland creatures being your cute woodland selves."

"But I'm not a woodland creature," Red said.

"Ever heard of *acting?*" said Pop. "Make like a squirrel, a frog, or a chipmunk. Just be natural. That's key."

"If you say so." Red took her place with Bobby behind the pigs and put down her basket.

"Action!" the weasel cried, and the pigs began discussing plans to build a state-of-the-art barn for a client whose name they could not reveal. The project seemed very mysterious.

Everything went fine until the sound guy—a hare—yanked off his headset. "I'm picking up some kind of *flapping* noises here."

"Cut!" said the weasel. "Who's flapping?"

No one answered. The hare adjusted his headset and listened again. "Okay, it's gone. But see that it doesn't happen again."

"A-a-a-and—*action!*" said Pop. But the word was

barely out of his mouth when the hare yanked off his headset again.

This time it wasn't flapping. This time someone had shrieked.

The someone was Little Red Hoodie herself!

EIGHT

Eeeek! A Spider!

"Now what?" the weasel snapped.

"Snack break?" asked the littlest pig.

"I sure could use a smidge of slops," said the biggest pig.

"You boys won't fit into your wardrobe at this rate," said Ratón Perez.

"Just what is it about porky that you don't understand?" asked the littlest pig.

"This is not a snack break!" said Pop. "We can't shoot with someone shrieking. You, there—Teal,

Magenta, Turquoise—whatever your name is. What in the woods is the problem?"

"My basket of goodies is gone!" I said.

"Basket of goodies?" said the littlest pig. "Where?"

"Was there banana bread?" asked the middle-sized pig. "We pigs love banana bread."

"Just exactly what *was* in that basket?" Bobby Bear asked, not for the first time.

I was ready to answer when something surprising happened.

What? What?

A spider dropped down from the branch of a fir tree and landed smack-dab on her hoodie!

Now it was Bobby Bear's turn to shriek.

That spider was the size of Papa Bear's paw! And he was black and hairy and big-toothed!

Arthropods don't even have teeth, Bobby. They chew their food with their mandibles. As if spider jaws aren't scary?

Soon just about everyone on the TV crew, pigs included, was squealing:

Eeeek!

Squish it!

I just rolled my eyes and muttered, "Bunch o' babies," before greeting the spider politely and asking its name.

"Anansi's my name and tricks are my game," said the spider. "What's with the long face, little girl?"

"I've lost my last goodie basket," I said. "Did one of your eight eyes happen to see what happened?"

"Oh, sure. I saw," Anansi said. "It was the furry guy beside you. He stole your basket! I saw the whole thing!"

NINE

The True Meaning of Spider Snot

Red looked daggers at me and said, "How could you?"

"Looked daggers" means gave him a look so mean it would have cut him to shreds if looks could cut you to shreds.

"I didn't!" I said.

"Did, too!" the spider said.

"If I took it—and I didn't—what did I do with it?" I asked.

"You ate the goodies and tossed the basket into the shrubbery," Anansi said.

"Wait—were there cookies in the basket?" I asked.

"Of course," Anansi said. "Who ever heard of a basket of goodies without cookies?"

"In that case, it's better that I tossed the basket than tossed the cookies—right?" I said.

Very funny, Bobby.

Hahaha! I got a million of 'em. But getting back to the story: Anansi, that tricky spider, and I argued a bit, which was boring, and finally I won the argument because (1) I was telling the truth and he was lying, and (2) I am the main character of the story and he is just a bit player.

Say what? Bit player? I want a new contract! Where's my agent?

How did you get here?

One thing spiders are good at is hiding out and spying.

Well, one thing *spies* are good at is keeping quiet. You should give it a try. Now, where was I? Oh, yes. I was exasperated!

"Who are you gonna believe," I asked Red, "a cute, furry mammal such as myself, or an icky, creepy multi-legged arthropod?"

Red looked pained. "Not every mammal is a good guy, Bobby Bear, while many spiders are interesting and beautiful."

Hearing that, Anansi made a strange, choking sound.

"Oh, dear—are you crying?" Red asked him.

"He's faking," I said.

"Am not," Anansi sniffed.

Ewww—spider snot! Think how disgusting that would be!

Enough!

No, he wasn't. "Hardly anyone says spiders are interesting and beautiful," he explained. "So, from the bottom of my heart and speaking for spiders everywhere, I just want to say thank you to Red for the kind words."

"You're quite welcome," Red said. "Now, please tell us who stole my basket? No more tricks."

"It was the biggest pig brother!" Anansi said.

Red and I shook our heads.

"The medium-sized pig brother?" Anansi tried.

Red and I shook our heads again. "All three pig brothers were in plain sight the whole time."

"Oh, fine," Anansi admitted. "The fact is I have no idea, but right before I heard Red shriek, I heard a sound like flapping."

"The rabbit heard flapping, too," Red said thoughtfully.

Anansi prepared to depart. "If you'll excuse me, I got a waterspout to climb before it rains."

"But there's not a cloud in the sky," Red said.

"Then I gotta go up the spout again," said Anansi. "Good luck!"

TEN

Are You Trying to Scare Me?

I made a calculation.

So far, the bear cub and I had walked approximately 10 yards. At that rate, I would deliver the basket right about Christmastime . . . in the year 3000.

"We need to hurry," I told Bobby.

But Bobby did not move. "What's the point in going to the castle without goodies? How about you go home, bake more and come back. Feel free to drop by the tidy cottage anytime and knock on the door. If I'm home . . . I'll run out the back as fast as I can."

"You're not a bit amusing."
I said.

> Not amusing? You are looking at the three-time winner of *The Woods Got Talent* stand-up comedy large predator junior division.

And just how many contestants were there in the large predator junior division, Bobby?

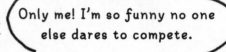

> Only me! I'm so funny no one else dares to compete.

"I am going to the castle—basket or no. I must see my grandmother and tell her what happened," Red said.

"Oh, all right," said Bobby. "You can't go by yourself."

The morning was late by this time. Sunbeams dappled the forest floor as the scent of sap perfumed the air.

Bobby and Red trod
past the pond where the
turtle played her harp, the blueberry patch favored by
Cock Robin, and eventually Coyote's den.

At last, they reached the outskirts of civilization,
woods style, where the trees were fewer and the rocks
more numerous.

Red was brave and determined but unaccustomed to so much hiking. "How much farther?" she asked, breathlessly. "Uh . . . asking for a friend."

"Up over the pass, down into the valley of death, and then we're there," Bobby said.

"Valley of death?"

Bobby shrugged. "It feels that way—what with the vultures and the flying monkeys and all. But don't worry. I'm sure your grandma the queen is probably a perfectly nice person, only evil Monday through Sunday, mostly misunderstood."

"Are you trying to scare me?" Red asked.

Bobby shrugged. "I'm not the one who took my eye off the goodie basket. By the way, what was in it anyway? Besides baked goods, I mean."

"It doesn't matter now." Red sighed. "The goodies are gone, and so are they."

"Who are *they*?" said Bobby.

"Well, if you must know," Red began, but before she could say more, she was interrupted by the *cheep-cheep-cheep* of a very agitated chick crossing the path ahead.

ELEVEN

The Sky Is Falling!

This sounds like one of those "why does the chicken cross the road?" riddles.

It wasn't though. It was totally different. For one thing, it wasn't a chicken, it was a chick. And for another, it wasn't a road, it was a path.

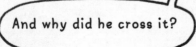
And why did he cross it?

He was trying to get to the king.

The king? What king? Since when is there a king?

Patience, my good Red. Patience. All will be revealed in time.

Ha! I guess I deserved that one.

Ha! I guess you did.

Meanwhile, the chick kept right on cheeping. "The sky is falling! The sky is falling! And I must run to tell the king!"

Little Red looked up into the sky, which was blue and cloudless. "How do you know the sky is falling?" she asked.

"A piece of it hit me right in the head!" The agitated chick used his wing to demonstrate . . . and almost knocked himself flat.

"Oh dear, are you all right?" Red asked.

"Where am I?" asked the chick.

"On the path to the castle," Red said. "You were going to tell the king about the sky, only there isn't any king, there's only a queen."

"In that case I'll tell *her*," said the chick.

"I'd stay away from the queen if I were you," I said. "She's terrifying and evil."

"Or possibly misunderstood," Red said.

"*Cheep-cheep-cheep!*" said the chick. "The sky won't be falling all day, you know. I must get to the castle!"

"I am going there, too," Red said. "You're welcome to come along if you'd like. My name is Little Red Hoodie, and this is Bobby Bear."

"Chicken Little's my name. Catastrophe's my game. *Cheep-cheep-cheep!*"

Were you concerned we might've made a mistake inviting him along?

Oh boy, was I! Compared to *cheep-cheep-cheep,* the valley of death was starting to look good.

TWELVE

Barnyard Reunion

Bobby Bear, Little Red Hoodie, and Chicken Little continued down the path toward the castle.

"Tell me, Chicken Little," I said. "How did you come to live in the woods? Don't chickens usually live in barnyards?"

"Got that right," said the chick. "Thing is, I escaped."

> Escape from the Barnyard—good title for an action flick. I wonder if there were helicopters, fast cars, and sirens?

If so, he didn't mention it.

"And just why did you escape, if you don't mind my asking?" I asked.

"Sunday dinner was coming, and some of us were getting nervous—if you know what I mean. The Pig Brothers built a tunnel under the fence, and everyone followed them out. Soon the rest of the domestic fowl and I had new digs in the woods. Why look—there's Henny Penny now! I must tell her my news!"

Sure enough, a well-dressed red hen was pecking in the dirt ahead.

"Cheep-cheep-*cheep*! The sky is falling!" Chicken Little cried.

The hen did not look up. "Last time you thought the sun had burned out when it was actually behind a cloud."

"This time it's for real! Cheep-cheep-*cheep*!"

"OMG, would you stop with the cheeping! I've known less annoying smoke detectors," Henny Penny said. "Who are your friends? Where are you going?"

Bobby Bear and I introduced ourselves and explained.

"I've never seen a castle," Henny Penny said. "A big red barn is more my style. Still, I wouldn't mind a walk. May I come with you?"

Chicken Little, Henny Penny, Bobby Bear, and Little Red Hoodie continued, the path. Soon they came upon another of Chicken Little's friends.

"The sky is falling! The sky is falling!" Chicken Little told Goosey Loosey.

It was like a barnyard reunion!

Goosey Loosey had been doing calisthenics. Now she tucked in her wings and said, "What is it now, Chicken? I seem to remember the last time it rained, you suggested we build an ark."

"And remember when there was that little bit of sleet and he sang the entire score from *Frozen*?" Henny Penny asked.

"Laugh all you want, but the sky *is* falling," Chicken Little said. "And I am going to the castle to tell the king."

"You mean the queen," Bobby Bear said, "and she's evil. Just sayin'."

"There's some misunderstanding," I said.

"I could use a walk," said Goosey Loosey.

So Goosey Loosey, Henny Penny, Chicken Little, Bobby Bear, and Little Red Hoodie continued on the path. And you'll never guess who they met next.

Rhymes with herky-jerky?

Okay, maybe you will guess.

There by the side of the path was Turkey-Lurky, shaking her tail feathers and wiggling her wattle. "Happ'nin', Chick?" she said.

"The sky is falling! The sky is falling!" cried Chicken Little.

"Come with us," said Goosey Loosey. "The chick'll never let you rest until you do."

So Turkey Lurky, Goosey Loosey, Henny Penny, Chicken Little, Bobby Bear, Little Red Hoodie, and Foxy Loxy continued on the path toward the castle—

65

THIRTEEN

Free All-You-Can-Eat Buffet

All along, Foxy Loxy had been lurking nearby unseen. Now, quietly, he joined the little band on the path.

The temperature dropped. The fog rolled in. Vultures circled overhead. Also flying monkeys. When the castle came into view, it was tall, it was dark, it was—

Handsome?

No, not handsome.

Spooky!

"Cheep-cheep-*cheep*!" cried Chicken Little. For once, he spoke for everybody.

"Does the king live in th-th-there?" Henny Penny asked

"Because if so, you're on your own, Chicken Little," said Goosey Lucy.

"Catch ya on the flip side," said Turkey Lurky.

"Not the king. The queen. *She* lives in there," I said.

"The bear's been trying to explain that for a while, you know," Red said.

Foxy Loxy spoke at last: "Bobby Bear is absolutely right. It's the queen who lives in the tall, dark, spooky castle. The king, on the other hand, is a hospitable fellow who lives in a sweet palace packed with all the feed a fowl could ever desire. Would you like to visit him? Come right this way."

With his tail, the fox pointed toward a cave entrance that looked a lot like a fox den.

Chicken Little, Henny Penny, Goosey Loosey and Turkey Lurky hesitated.

Foxy Loxy spoke up again, "Oh, and I forgot to mention: Free all-you-can-eat buffet every day at noon."

"What time is it now?" asked Chicken Little.

"Five of," said Foxy Loxy. "Better hurry."

With a great kerfuffle of feathers, the barnyard fowl moved toward the (pick one) fox den/secret passage to the king's buffet.

"Wait!" I cried. "Think before you act!"

"No time to think!" cried Chicken Little. "The sky is falling! Also: Lunchtime. Cheep-cheep-*cheep*!"

One by one, the birds disappeared. Behind them followed Foxy Loxy himself, waving his red tail like a flag.

FOURTEEN

I Will Bean That Birdbrain

For a few moments it was quiet, and then from inside the cave came a terrible noise: yipping, squawking, honking, gobbling, and cheep-cheep-*cheep*ing all at once!

Bobby Bear sighed. "He was an annoying chick, and a dumb chick, but not a bad chick."

Then—abruptly—a jumble of feathers, beaks, and drumsticks exploded from the hillside onto the path.

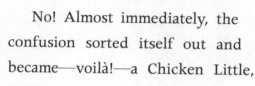

What the heck? Were our new friends in fragments?

No! Almost immediately, the confusion sorted itself out and became—voilà!—a Chicken Little, Henny Penny, Goosey Loosey, and Turkey Lurky, each one gawping and gaping in surprise.

As Bobby Bear and Little Red Hoodie tried to take all this in, two more objects burst from the hillside: first, a red-hot fireball sparking and smoking in the sun; and then, almost as bright, a flash of red tail, black paws, and sharp teeth.

Was it Foxy Loxy?

No, it was not. Don't you remember? It was *Mrs.* Foxy Loxy, also known as Kitsune. Juggling fireballs is her talent.

". . . and stay out!" she yipped.

"Keep her away! Keep her away!" cried the fowl.

"You woke the kits from their nap!" said Kitsune sternly. "Do you know how long it's going to take me to get them settled again? And there's dusting to do and laundry and grocery hunting . . ."

"It wasn't our fault!" chirped Chicken Little. "Foxy Loxy was taking us to the king!"

"I will bean that birdbrain when I get hold of him," said Kitsune. "Just once I'd like to see *him* get the kits down for nap."

Abashed, Foxy Loxy himself emerged from the cave. "I had the best of intentions," he claimed.

Little Red Hoodie was ready to move on. "This has all been very interesting," she said. "But now we must continue on our way to the castle."

"But what about the king?" asked Chicken Little.

"And the king's buffet?" said Henny Penny.

Foxy Loxy tried again. "If you and your delicious — that is, *attractive*—friends will just follow me . . ."

"Oh, no, you don't," said Kitsune. "You get right back in there and watch your children. I have an appointment for a pawdicure."

> I get it! Pawdicure instead of pedicure!

Sometimes, Bobby, you are a genius.

> In that case, may I take a turn telling the story?

Be my guest.

FIFTEEN

What Ho!

The castle was still tall, dark, and spooky when Chicken Little, Henny Penny, Goosey Loosey, Turkey Lurky, Little Red Hoodie, and I approached.

I was trembling. I was scared. I was getting ready to say goodbye (forever?) to Little Red Hoodie.

As for the barnyard fowl, I could see by their beady little eyes that they were scared, too.

And what with the vultures and flying monkeys and all, the sound of flapping was everywhere.

Flapping. That reminds me of something . . .

I know, right?

But before any of us could reflect on such an important clue, a piece fell from the sky, bounced off Little Red Hoodie's head, and landed in the path.

"Ouch!" said Little Red Hoodie.

"Cheep-cheep-*cheep*!" cried Chicken Little. "Told ya!"

Red picked up the piece of sky, turned it over in her hands, and studied it.

"Why does the sky look like homemade banana bread?" she asked.

"I don't know," I said. "Why *does* the sky look like homemade banana bread?"

"It's not a riddle, Bobby," said Red. "Here. Take a look."

I took the item, studied it, sniffed it, ate it.

"I love banana bread," I said . . . just as a large wicker basket caught on a tree branch above, did a little jig, and fell to the ground beside us.

"My goodie basket—hooray!" cried Red.

We grabbed for it at the same time.

"I'm just going to take the tiniest peek," I grunted.

"Nothing in there but goodies, only goodies," Red said.

The tug-of-war was a standoff. We glared at each . . . then something unexpected happened.

Yes, again. If you think of it, that's kind of how stories work. Things happen, many of them unexpected. Otherwise no one would keep reading.

A voice spoke up. It was human. It seemed to be male. And it did not come from inside the castle.

Or the basket.

"What ho, woodland creatures, barnyard fowl, and human child! What brings you to the castle?"

SIXTEEN

An Infestation of Humans

The voice belonged to a big, burly, bearded guy who appeared a moment later.

"The king!" said Chicken Little. "Didn't I tell you?"

"I am not the king," said the man.

"But you're human, have straight teeth, and hang around the castle. Who else would you be?" Chicken Little asked. "Did I mention the sky is falling?"

The big, burly, bearded guy scratched his head, which, by the way, was crown-free.

"Hmmm," he said, "let me think. I have a woods-man's ax over my shoulder. I am wearing a flannel woodsman's shirt and canvas woodsman's pants. Who do *you* think I am?"

With a lot of clucking, quacking, honking, and gob-bling, the barnyard fowl discussed the question. Finally, Chicken Little asked, "Can we have one more hint?"

The big, burly guy pulled out his wallet and showed a membership card in the Modern Woodsmen of America.

The fowl studied this and discussed some more. At last Chicken Little repeated: "The king!"

"It's unanimous," Henny Penny added.

"I'm actually a woodsman," said the woodsman.

"That was my next guess," said Chicken Little.

"So, if you're not the king," said Bobby Bear, "what are you doing here?"

"I live here," he explained, "but not in the castle. In fact, I have my own little hovel out back. Soon, though—"

The woodsman was going to say more but, at that very moment, someone poked her head above the par-apet.

"Hello-o-o-o down there! How ya doin'? Come around to the back door, and I'll let you in."

"Goldilocks!" cried Bobby Bear. "What are you doing here?"

SEVENTEEN

There's Something Funny Going On

"I'm here waiting for you, Bobby Bear," Goldilocks explained—after Chicken Little, Henny Penny, Goosey Loosey, Turkey Lurky, the woodsman, Bobby Bear, and Little Red Hoodie had passed through the back door, stood around awestruck by the stony, cold, cavernous castle, and had been introduced.

"I had some news for Bobby Bear, so I walked from my house in the burbs to the tidy cottage," Goldilocks continued. "Mama Bear and Papa Bear had company, but Ratón Perez told me where you'd gone, and I hightailed it here. No offense, but I knew you could never handle the evil queen on your own. Sheesh, you guys sure took your time."

> We should have asked her what her news was.

Not to mention the identity of Mama and Papa Bear's company. But other questions seemed more important at that moment.

"How did you get into the castle, Furless?" Bobby Bear asked. "And what made you think you'd be safe from the evil queen?"

"What can I say? I'm naturally lucky," said Goldilocks. "When I got to the castle, the first thing I saw was a sign tacked to the mailbox: *On vacation far away. Please hold deliveries. Sincerely, The Evil Queen.* Then I saw someone had left the drawbridge open. Since the queen was gone, I strolled over the moat and came on in."

The woodsman frowned. "I've known the queen for years, and she never goes on vacation. If you ask me, there's something funny going on."

"It isn't funny to me," I said. "I've come all this way and my grandmother isn't even here!"

Goldilocks put a hand on my shoulder. "I know how you feel," she said. "I suffered a big disappointment in this very same castle one time."

She meant the first story about me.

The first story about *her*, you mean, the one that made Goldilocks famous throughout the burbs.

"Besides, *somebody's* still here," Goldilocks went on. "I didn't get a good look, but she's furry, she's got a big nose, she's wearing a pink nightie, and she's dozing in the guest bedroom upstairs."

"Cheep-cheep-*cheep*!" cried Chicken Little. "Whoever it is is good enough for me. And now I must run to tell her the sky is falling!"

"Wait!" cried Henny Penny, Goosey Loosey, Turkey Lurky, Bobby Bear, Little Red Hoodie, the woodsman, and Goldilocks.

But it was too late. Chicken Little was on a mission. And before anyone could stop him, he had ascended the narrow, dark, twisting, stone stairs.

"I don't like the sound of this," said the woodsman, who was turning out to be rather a gloomy Gus. "Furry with a long nose makes me think of the Big Bad Wolf."

"The Wolf always struck me as more the blue plaid jammies type," said Bobby Bear.

"A clever disguise?" said the woodsman.

Bobby Bear slapped paw to forehead. "Then that chick is about to be snack food! Come on—we have to hurry!"

EIGHTEEN

Granny, Are You Snarling?

With a lot of fluttering, squawking, honking, gobbling, and hubbub, Henny Penny, Goosey Loosey, Turkey Lurky, the woodsman, Goldilocks, and I burst into the guest bedroom.

Wait, what happened to me?

You got lost on the way.

Oh, yes. There was an orb weaver on the stairs. I stopped to have a look and somehow got turned around. What was in the guest bedroom?

Just like Goldilocks said, some furry guy with a long nose wearing a pink nightie got up from the bed. But that wasn't the scary part.

What was the scary part?

Clutched in the guy's mandibles was Chicken Little, cheep-cheep-*cheeping* for dear life!

As always, I thought fast: "Let him go, or the goodie basket gets it!"

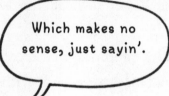
Which makes no sense, just sayin'.

Maybe not, but it worked. The furry guy opened his mouth to speak, and—cheep-cheep-*cheep*—Chicken Little flapped his way free and escaped.

"What goodie basket?" the furry guy asked. "Is there banana bread?"

At that very moment, Little Red Hoodie appeared in the doorway. "I've got the basket right here in my hand, but first may I ask who you are?"

"Why certainly, my dear," said the furry guy. "I am a kindly old granny."

"Perhaps," said Little Red. "But you're not *my* kindly old granny."

"I am, you know. Age and anxiety have altered my appearance. It happens to everyone. It will happen to you, too." The furry guy made a face.

Red looked the furry guy up and down. "Grandma," she said at last, "what big ears you have."

"The better to hear you with, my dear," said the furry guy.

"And, Grandma, what big eyes you have!" Red said.

"The better to see you with, my dear."

"And, Grandma, what big teeth you have!"

I don't like where this is going.

You are right to worry because with that, the furry guy leapt up, and the nightie dropped to the floor, revealing . . .

Grandma in her underwear?

. . . a shiny-pelted, red-eyed, fearsome-looking wolf!

NINETEEN

When Do I Get to Eat You?

"I knew it all along," said Goldilocks.

"Busted," the Wolf muttered, and then: "All the better to eat you with, my dear!"

When the Wolf lunged at me, Bobby blocked his path, so he flailed at everyone else at once. Flying fur! Flying feathers! Noise! Tumult! Upset!

At last, one sound cut through the chaos: "Cheep-cheep-*cheep*!"

Everyone froze. Everyone assessed their well-being. Miraculously, no one was hurt.

"Look, Mr. Wolf," I said breathlessly. "Maybe we can make a deal. I give you a loaf of banana bread. You go back to the woods. Act now, and the woodsman won't chop off your head."

"When do I get to eat you and all the little birdies, Tweet-Tweet?" the Wolf asked.

"You don't," said I.

"Not even the annoying little chicken?" the Wolf asked.

I thought for a moment.

"Hey!" Chicken Little protested.

I sighed. "No, not even the chicken."

Goldilocks raised a hand. "Hang on a sec." Then she whispered something in my ear.

My eyes opened wide. "He swallowed her in one gulp? But how do you know?"

"Library story hour," Goldilocks said.

"In that case, Mr. Woodsman, please do chop off his head!" I said.

"*Ewww*—think of the mess," said the woodsman, who proceeded to grab a handy yardstick, ask the wolf to open wide, and measure the space between his jaws. "No grandma would fit," the woodsman announced.

"Besides," said the Wolf, "she's an evil queen—remember? No way would I eat something so sour, so bitter, so toxic, so—"

I wonder how long he would have gone on.

No telling.

As it was, the litany was cut off by a loud *bang* from elsewhere in the castle: It was the drawbridge slamming shut!

And that's when the evil queen herself appeared.

"I thought you were on vacation," said Goldilocks.

The evil queen cackled her evil cackle, and what was worse, the Wolf joined in.

"I see you fell for our little trick, Goldilocks," the queen said.

"And now," said the Wolf, "every last one of you is trapped!"

TWENTY

To the Basement with You!

> All this time the evil queen and the Big Bad Wolf were working together.

You got it. They put the sign on the mailbox and opened the drawbridge so Goldilocks would think it was safe to come inside.

> And then, when all of us had come inside—slam!—the queen closed the drawbridge.

So the world-famous Goldilocks wasn't so smart after all.

Hey, we all make mistakes. Like for example, somebody held the map upside down.

I can't believe you're defending Goldilocks! I thought you were annoyed with her!

She was nice to me, and I got over it.

"You are now my prisoners," said the evil queen. "Off to the basement with you! March!"

Chicken Little, Henny Penny, Goosey Loosey, Turkey Lurky, Little Red Hoodie, the woodsman, Goldilocks, the Big Bad Wolf, and I marched down the narrow, dark, twisting stone stairs . . . and then down some more narrow, dark, twisting stone stairs.

"Uh, your majesty." The Big Bad Wolf dropped back
to whisper in her ear. "Surely you don't mean to take
me prisoner as well?"

"And why not?" the queen asked.

"Because you and I are allies in evil! No one can
stop us, not even the king of beasts. Soon all woodland
creatures will be our slaves. You've heard of world domination? This will be woods domination!"

Meanwhile, I, Bobby Bear, was talking to the woodsman. "Can't you do something? You are big and strong and burly. You have straight white teeth and an ax!"

"And you have sharp teeth and claws," said the woodsman. "But I don't see you stepping up. Face it. The Wolf and the queen are just too evil. Sometimes the good guys lose."

> Would this be one of those times?

There's only one way to find out.

> Keep reading!

TWENTY-ONE

What's in the Basket?

Where were we?

Narrow, dark, twisting
stone stairs.

That's right! I remember it
as if it were yesterday.

It was yesterday.

There you go then.

"I have an idea," I said.

"Do I have to cut off anyone's head?" asked the woodsman.

"No," I said. "Just follow my lead."

"I'm in," said the woodsman.

"Me too," said Chicken Little, Henny Penny, Goosey Loosey, Turkey Lurky, and Bobby Bear. The Big Bad Wolf and evil queen were too busy arguing to overhear.

At last they all arrived in the basement, which was also the laundry room. It was rather small and damp, altogether a gloomy place to be held prisoner—especially with barnyard fowl who had not been properly housebroken.

The Big Bad Wolf surveyed the situation. "Your majesty," he whimpered. "I can't possibly spend the rest of my life imprisoned here. What will I eat?"

The queen looked pointedly at Chicken Little, Henny Penny, Goosey Loosey, and Turkey Lurky. "Do you really need me to spell that out for you?"

"Is there ranch dressing?" the wolf asked.

"I'm not running a diner," said the queen. "You'll eat them plain or you won't eat them at all."

"Not eat them at all, that's my vote," said Henny Penny.

"Second," said Goosey Loosey.

"Speaking of diners, did I mention I'm carrying a goodie basket?" Little Red Hoodie, the main character, indeed we may say the *hero*, held up the goodie basket in case the queen required a visual cue.

"Wait, Red!" cried Goldilocks. "Don't give up the goodie basket! We'll starve!"

"Don't give up the goodie basket!" cried Chicken Little, Henny Penny, Goosey Loosey, Turkey Lurky, the woodsman, and Bobby Bear.

I rolled my eyes. "Chillax, people. It's all part of my good idea, okay?"

"Oh, right," said Henny Penny.

"Carry on," said Goosey Loosey.

"We cool," said Turkey Lurky.

"What good idea?" asked the Big Bad Wolf.

"Never you mind," said Red. "Now, your majesty, do you want the basket or not?"

"What's in it?" the queen asked.

"I'll show you," said Red.

Hooray! I've been waiting all this time for you to open the gosh-darned basket!

Red opened the lid of the basket, rummaged around and removed a wrapped-up loaf of banana bread. Immediately, the delicious smell filled the basement, making life seem not so bad after all.

The evil queen smacked her lips and drooled, but only a little. "I love banana bread," she declared.

 "Gimme that goodie basket!"

"Okeydoke," said Little Red Hoodie. "Catch!"

TWENTY-TWO

I Can't Believe What Was in the Basket!

The queen raised her bejeweled hands to catch the basket, but not quite quickly enough. The flying basket caught her—*bam!*—in the belly—"Oof!"—then it flipped over, fell to the floor and opened, spilling its contents everywhere.

For a moment the basement was still.

Then all at once everyone was clucking, gobbling, hissing, or growling.

Eeeek!

"Don't you dare!" I said.
"They're spiders and they're
only babies after all!"

Baby spiders *and* goodies.

Remember the special grandma gift I added before leaving my house?

The home décor?

Exactly! What's a house without cobwebs to make it homey? I happened to know about a sac of spider eggs in a dark corner of my closet. That was the goodie I added to the basket, and on the journey, the eggs must have hatched.

Now, in the castle basement, those spider babies crept and crawled everywhere in search of food and shelter, same as any other tiny creature. They had no opinion about evil queens, wolves, barnyard fowl, or furless girls. They only wanted to survive.

But the evil queen and the Big Bad Wolf thought the spiders were out to get them!

So they squealed and jumped and stomped. But the spiders were quick and escaped behind the washer-dryer where, no doubt, they are living happily ever after.

Meanwhile, in the midst of the hubbub and confusion, the woodsman said, "Follow me. I know a shortcut."

Soon Chicken Little, Henny Penny, Goosey Loosey, Turkey Lurky, Bobby Bear, Little Red Hoodie, the woodsman, and Goldilocks all stood in the main hall of the castle, which was decorated with brilliant tapestries, shiny gold candelabras, oil paintings of fairy-tale villains, and about a zillion cupboards, chests of drawers, bureaus, sideboards, and buffets.

Now Chicken Little, Henny Penny, Goosey—

We get it! The good guys!

The good guys, yes. The good guys had just one tiny problem.

How to escape the tall, dark, spooky castle!

Precisely.

TWENTY-THREE

We're Done For

So, there we all stood in the main hall of the castle, and Goldilocks turned to me, and just looked daggers!

We all remember what that means, do we not?

"I knew you should've kept that clicker!" Goldilocks said.

"You mean the clicker that opens the drawbridge? The one I returned to the evil queen in the first story?"

"Yes, Bobby Bear. *That* clicker," Goldilocks said.

"Goldilocks," I said patiently. "As you know, I am a good and careful little bear. I do not keep stolen property."

"What's a clicker?" asked Henny Penny.

"Hahaha! That's pretty funny coming from a clucker!" said Goldilocks. "Get it? She's a chicken, and chickens say—"

"I get it," I said.

"A clicker is the same as a remote control," Little Red Hoodie explained. "You know, like to open a garage door."

"Or a drawbridge," said the woodsman, who, with unerring swiftness, strode to one of the zillion cupboards and cabinets, opened one of the zillion drawers, and retrieved something. "I believe this is the item in question."

"That's it! I'd know that clicker anywhere!" said Bobby Bear.

"Click it! Click it! Click it!" everybody cried at once.

The woodsman did.

Nothing happened.

"Looking for these?" Behind us in the main hall, the evil queen appeared. Having rushed up the narrow, dark, twisting stone stairs, she was breathless. In her bejeweled hand she clasped some triple-A batteries.

"We're done for," said Chicken Little.

"Goodbye, cruel woods," said Henny Penny.

"What else ya got?" asked Turkey Lurky.

"Nada," said the woodsman with a sigh.

> This was a bad, bad moment. But then, in a surprise development, the queen spoke directly to the woodsman.

"I let you get away once," she told him. "I'm not letting you get away again. If you'll stay here with me, the others can leave."

"What's she talking about?" said Little Red Hoodie.

"Never mind details, I vote yes," said Henny Penny.

"All in favor?" said Goosey Loosey.

"Hey, hang on there!" the woodsman cried.

But then—

> Another unexpected development!

From the direction of the kitchen came a strange and echoing sound: *trip-trop, trip-trop, trip-trop.*

"Whatever it is, it's coming this way," said Chicken Little.

"I only hope it's on our side," said Goldilocks.

"Speak for yourself," said the evil queen at the same moment a large barnyard creature appeared in the hall. With its floppy ears, long beard and very pointy horns, it looked exactly like—

> —the largest Billy Goat Gruff!

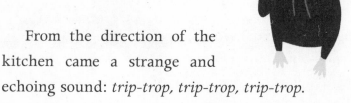

And that is who it was.

"I've followed the aroma of banana bread for hours," he said, "and I'm not leaving till I get some."

Little Red Hoodie opened the goodie basket. The baby spiders had been lost in the laundry room along with most of the goodies. But one loaf of banana bread remained. "You are welcome," she told the goat. "Do you happen to have any batteries?"

"What size?" the goat asked.

"Triple-A," said Little Red Hoodie.

"Fresh out," said the goat. "Why do you need them?"

Little Red Hoodie explained.

"That flimsy drawbridge there?" said the goat.

"Flimsy?" said the queen. "I'll have you know I hired the finest contractors in the woods, Discount Beavers R Us."

"Should've hired Pig Brothers," said the goat and then, without further ado, he lowered his horns, stomped his hooves, tossed his head, and charged!

Hinges busted, the drawbridge dropped, and—*trip-trop, trip-trop*—the goat led the way as the good guys crossed to safety.

TWENTY-FOUR

Questions for the Woodsman

But how safe was it really?

Wasn't the evil queen right there ready to cross the moat herself, round everyone up with help from flying monkeys, and march them down to the laundry room?

Nope. The queen was much too busy.

Exactly right. She was on the phone with Discount Beavers R Us, demanding her money back.

As for the biggest Billy Goat Gruff, Little Red Hoodie gave him the last loaf of banana bread, which he devoured in one bite.

"I love banana bread," he said, and smacked his lips and *trip-trop trip-tropped* toward home.

Meanwhile, there were questions for the woodsman, such as why the evil queen offered to trade him for the rest of them.

And how had he known where she kept the clicker?

The woodsman's response was a sigh. "Once upon a time I lived in the castle with the queen, which is why I know about its shortcuts and clickers. As for why she offered to trade, I can't say. Maybe she misses me?"

"Do you miss her?" Goldilocks asked.

"Perhaps you hadn't noticed, but she's evil," said

the woodsman emphatically. "Would any of you care to live in a castle with her?"

"No!" said Chicken Little, Henny Penny, Goosey Loosey, Turkey Lurky, Bobby Bear, Little Red Hoodie, and Goldilocks.

"Wait a second," Goldilocks added. "If you lived in the castle, does that mean . . . ?"

The woodsman nodded. "It means I used to be king."

Henny Penny, Goosey Loosey, Turkey Lurky, Goldilocks, Bobby Bear, and Little Red were so surprised, they gasped.

As for Chicken Little, this was the chance he'd been waiting for: "Cheep-cheep-*cheep*! The sky is falling!"

TWENTY-FIVE

The King's Story, a Digression

Once upon a time . . .

You said that already.

Does she always interrupt like this?

Once upon a time there was a tall, good-looking boy with straight teeth who happened to be the son of a king and queen in a faraway land.

From the woods, of course. On the plus side, it did have good freeway access.

The tall, good-looking boy had a pleasant disposition and seldom got in trouble—except for that one time.

What happened that one time?

He received an ax as a gift for his birthday and chopped down a tree, not realizing till too late that woodland creatures relied on it for food and shelter.

Mostly the woodland creatures were kind to the boy who was kind to them. But they got mad when he axed the tree, and he felt very bad.

Over time the prince grew from a tall, good-looking boy to a tall, good-looking man . . .

If you do say so yourself . . .

. . . and married the princess who lived in the castle in the faraway woods.

More time passed, and the prince and princess became the king and queen.

But now the king had a secret. He was not happy. In fact, he didn't like being king at all.

Why not? It sounds like a good gig.

But the worst problem was the queen. She was bossy, bad-tempered, and greedy. She wore too much eye makeup. Some might even have called her evil!

One day the queen, who was in the parlor eating bread and honey, ordered the king to get himself down to the counting house and commence to count out his money.

"I hate counting money!" he said—but quietly so the bad-tempered queen could not hear. "Maybe I should do something else with my life."

Looking back, he remembered one happy time: the birthday when he chopped down the tree.

So the king went online and ordered an ax. When

it arrived, he announced he was quitting, hoisted the ax over his shoulder, used the clicker to open the drawbridge, crossed the moat, and started his new life as a woodsman in a hovel behind the tall, dark, spooky castle.

Whoa—seriously? And did he live happily ever after?

Unfortunately not. He was forever arguing with woodland creatures about the whole tree-chopping business. So, he decided to try farming, and he hired some guys to build a barn.

You mean Discount Beavers R Us?

No, he went whole hog.

In other words—

He hired the world-famous Pig Brothers!

He must have had some king money set aside.

As we speak, the barn is under construction. All that's needed are a few barnyard animals to make this ex-king's dream a reality.

TWENTY-SIX

I Love Banana Bread

As the ex-king told his story, Chicken Little looked thoughtful, or as close to thoughtful as a chick ever looks. "So, your highness, I told you the sky is falling, right?"

The woodsman cringed. "Please don't call me your highness. It makes me cringe."

"I see that," said Chicken Little. "But you're the next best thing, and my job was to tell the king the sky is falling. So I did. And it's disappointing that you don't even care."

"The sky is not falling," said the woodsman. "I work outside, and if it were, I would have seen bits and pieces."

"If it's not falling," said the chick, "how do you explain this?" He untucked a wing to reveal a lump of bread, or possibly cake. "It fell from the sky this morning, and conked me right in the head!"

"Shouldn't it be blue?" asked Henny Penny.

"Or white like a cloud?" asked Goosey Loosey.

"I wonder if it's gluten-free," said Goldilocks. "Because it smells like—"

"—*banana bread!*" Everyone chorused at once.

"I love banana bread," I said. "It's so much better than porridge."

"You know," said Red, "This looks exactly like one of my mama's banana breads. But how could it possibly have made its way up into the sky?"

"Or down upon my head?" said Chicken Little.

"It's a mystery all right," I said as, overhead, flying monkeys made monkey noises and loudly flapped their wings.

We might have discussed the question further. We might even have solved the mystery. But before we could, we were startled by a terrible noise, one that struck fear into our hearts and, in some cases, gizzards.

Aw-roohr!

TWENTY-SEVEN

Which One Shall I Eat First?

Was it the wolf?

Well, it wasn't the Pig Brothers!

Someone—I'm not naming names—had left the drawbridge open. Now we turned and saw that the Wolf himself was charging in our direction!

I clicked the clicker in a hurry, and the drawbridge began to rise. Higher and higher it went, so that the

Wolf's claws lost traction, and he slipped backward. With no other choice, he leapt for it and landed—*splash!*—in the moat.

Luckily? Whose side are you on?

A moment later, the Wolf emerged, dripping wet, muddy, and pathetic.

"I had to get out of there!" he said. "That queen is too evil even for me. I mean, it was lunchtime and all she offered me was a gnarly old apple. Not even blackbird pie."

"Let me get this straight," said Bobby Bear. "You escaped from the castle because you didn't want an apple for lunch?"

"A gnarly *old* apple," the Wolf clarified. "Did I mention I'm still hungry? And it's still lunchtime."

The wolf stared intently at the barnyard fowl.

"Not this again," said Bobby Bear. Then he turned to the woodsman who once had been a king. "Can't you do something?"

"What did you have in mind?" the woodsman asked.

"Raise yourself up to your full height, give the wolf a steely look of determination, and brandish your ax!" said Bobby Bear.

"Like this?" The woodsman followed directions, but the effect was not what Bobby had hoped.

The woodsman looked like a kid playing dress-up. Turns out there's not a fierce bone in his body.

Meanwhile, the wolf's fur had dried. He was no longer pathetic. He was shiny-pelted, red-eyed, and fearsome-looking. And he spoke in his snarliest, growliest voice: "Which one shall I eat first?"

TWENTY-EIGHT

Grrrr!

The Wolf advanced. Henny Penny, Goosey Loosey, Turkey Lurky, Bobby Bear, Little Red Hoodie, the woodsman, and Goldilocks cowered.

What *about* Chicken Little!

To everyone's surprise, he spoke up: "If you want one of us, you'll have to take all of us."

"Wait, what?" said Bobby Bear. "Since when is the tiny cheep-cheep-*cheep*er so brave?"

"Since I found out the sky's not falling," said Chicken Little. "Compared to that, what's a few sharp wolf teeth more or less?"

Bobby Bear was impressed, but the wolf stayed focused on mealtime. "Sounds like an all-you-can-eat buffet," he growled. "*Grrrr!*"

"*Grrrr!*" replied Chicken Little.

It was a great moment in fairy-tale history.

It sure was!

Never before had a menu item growled back at the Big Bad Wolf. Surprised, the Wolf hesitated, and Henny Penny, Goosey Loosey, Turkey Lurky, Bobby Bear, Little Red Hoodie, the woodsman, and Goldilocks took heart.

"Grrrr!" they chorused.

They had found their inner fierce!

They had indeed.

And now, for the first time, the Wolf noted Chicken Little's sharp little beak, Bobby Bear's sharp teeth and claws, and the woodsman's sharp blade. Maybe, he thought to himself, there's a less troublesome lunch option elsewhere in the woods.

But he couldn't simply turn tail and leave. That would be embarrassing. So he played the oldest trick in the storybook.

"Wait—what's that up there?!" he asked, looking toward the sky and gesturing with his paw.

Chicken Little, Henny Penny, Goosey Loosey, Turkey Lurky, Bobby Bear, Little Red Hoodie, the woodsman, and Goldilocks all looked. "Up where?" they asked, but there was nothing to see.

And when they looked back down, the Big Bad Wolf was gone.

TWENTY-NINE

Pig Brothers Are on TV

Chicken Little, Henny Penny, Goosey Loosey, and Turkey Lurky had a confab and decided that life in the woods was stressful. Homesick for regular mealtimes, they inked an agreement with the king-turned-woodsman-about-to-turn-farmer.

For their part, they would stick around the farm looking good and making all appropriate barnyard noises. For his part, he would not eat them for Sunday dinner.

As for Bobby Bear, Goldilocks, and me—we returned to the tidy cottage, eager to tell our story to Mama and Papa Bear.

But when we arrived, we saw that Mama and Papa Bear had company.

Who was it?

The troll that used to live under the bridge!

The one who used to guard the woods?

The very one!

It was he who had made the *thump-thrash* noise that lured Mama and Papa out of the tidy cottage way back on page 30.

Like the Billy Goats Gruff, he had followed the smell of banana bread. But once he got to talking with Mama and Papa . . . well, you know how grownups are.

Talk-talk-talk.
Yak-yak-yak.

Next thing, they were best friends hanging out in the parlor watching TV.

"*Shhh!*" said Papa when Goldilocks, Little Red Hoodie, and Bobby Bear entered.

"Pig Brothers are on," said the troll.

"We never miss it," said Mama. So what could Bobby Bear, Goldilocks, and Little Red Hoodie do? They sat down to watch the Pig Brothers, too. The episode was the one about the woodsman's barn, shot that very morning, featuring Bobby and Red in the background playing cute little woodland creatures.

"You look good," Mama told them.

"Very natural," the troll said.

Then all at once, everyone in the parlor gasped.

"What's that flying monkey doing there?" said Mama.

THIRTY

Two Astonishing Things in One Chapter

I knew the flapping was a clue!

The millions of kids reading this book knew that, too. Right, readers?

But did they know the flying monkey stole my basket?

They do now.

As the Pig Brothers discussed the fine points of barn-building, a flying monkey swooped down behind them, grabbed Red's basket of goodies, and flew away.

"Another mystery solved," said Goldilocks as the episode wrapped up and the credits rolled. "Uh, is anyone else starving?"

"One guess what's for supper," said Mama Bear.

At night, the woods get scary.

So Mama, Papa, and I invited Little Red Hoodie and Goldilocks to sleep over and go home in the morning.

"Great idea!" said Goldilocks. "The new baby is a terrible sleeper. I'll be much more comfortable here."

"New baby?" I repeated.

Goldilocks slapped her forehead. "I forgot to tell you! That was my news—the reason I came to visit. I have a baby sister, born last week. She's cute when she's not crying."

"Congratulations!" Red said to Goldilocks. "And thanks awfully for the invitation, Bobby, but I can't possibly stay. My mother would worry."

"So phone her," said Mama Bear.

"Wait—you have a phone?" said Little Red Hoodie.

"Of course!" said Mama Bear. "What do you think— we're barBEARians?"

"Hahaha—good one, Mama," I said.

"You're not the only comedian in the family, you know," said Mama.

When Red phoned home, she learned something astonishing.

Along with the baby, that makes two astonishing things in one chapter!

But who's counting, right?

"I am in the wrong woods altogether!" Red explained.

"That's what comes of holding the map upside down," I said.

"So your grandma was never an evil queen?" Goldilocks said. "She never lived in a tall, dark, spooky castle?"

"She lives in a humble cottage," Red said. "Mama promised to draw a new map. And anyway, she says I can't miss it. The humble cottage is the only one like it anywhere. Instead of wood or bricks, its walls are made of gingerbread."

"Yummy!" I said.

"Yummy!" said Goldilocks. "Maybe we can bake some more banana bread and all go visit her together."

DON'T FORGET TO READ
GOLDILOCKS, GO HOME!

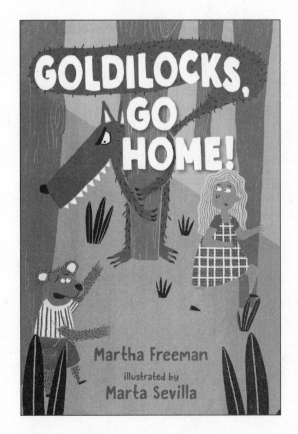